Every new generation of children is enthralled by the famous stories in our Well-Loved Tales series. Younger ones love to have the story read to them, and to examine each tiny detail of the full colour illustrations. Older children will enjoy the exciting stories in an easy-to-read text.

Goldilocks
and the
Three Bears

retold by **VERA SOUTHGATE** M A B Com
with illustrations by **ERIC WINTER**

Ladybird Books Loughborough

GOLDILOCKS
and the THREE BEARS

Once upon a time there were three bears who lived in a little house in a wood. Father Bear was a very big bear. Mother Bear was a medium-sized bear. Baby Bear was just a tiny, little bear.

One morning, Mother Bear cooked some porridge for breakfast. She put it into three bowls. There was a very big bowl for Father Bear, a medium-sized bowl for Mother Bear and a tiny, little bowl for Baby Bear.

The porridge was rather hot, so the three bears went for a walk in the wood, while it cooled.

Now at the edge of the wood, in another little house, there lived a little girl. Her golden hair was so long that she could sit on it. She was called Goldilocks.

On that very same morning, before breakfast, Goldilocks went for a walk in the wood.

Soon Goldilocks came to the little house where the three bears lived. The door was open and she peeped inside. No-one was there so she walked in.

Goldilocks saw the three bowls of porridge and the three spoons on the table. The porridge smelt good, and Goldilocks was hungry because she had not had her breakfast.

Goldilocks picked up the very big spoon and tasted the porridge in the very big bowl. It was too hot!

Then she picked up the medium-sized spoon and tasted the porridge in the medium-sized bowl. It was lumpy!

Then she picked up the tiny, little spoon and tasted the porridge in the tiny, little bowl. It was just right!

Soon she had eaten it all up!

Then Goldilocks saw three chairs; a very big chair, a medium-sized chair and a tiny, little chair.

She sat in the very big chair. It was too high!

She sat in the medium-sized chair. It was too hard!

Then she sat in the tiny, little chair. It was just right!

But was the tiny, little chair just right? No! Goldilocks was rather too heavy for it. The seat began to crack and then it broke.

Oh dear! Goldilocks had broken the tiny, little chair and she was so sorry.

Next Goldilocks went into the bedroom. There she saw three beds; a very big bed, a medium-sized bed and a tiny, little bed.

She felt tired and thought she would like to sleep.

So Goldilocks climbed up onto the very big bed. It was too hard!

Then she climbed up onto the medium-sized bed. It was too soft!

Then Goldilocks lay down on the tiny, little bed. It was just right!

Soon she was fast asleep.

Soon the three bears came home for breakfast.

Father Bear looked at his very big porridge bowl and said in a very loud voice, "Who has been eating *my* porridge?"

Mother Bear looked at her medium-sized porridge bowl and said in a medium-sized voice, "Who has been eating *my* porridge?"

Baby Bear looked at his tiny, little porridge bowl and said in a tiny, little voice, "Who has been eating *my* porridge and eaten it all up?"

Next Father Bear looked at his very big chair. "Who has been sitting in *my* chair?" he asked in a very loud voice.

Then Mother Bear looked at her medium-sized chair. "Who has been sitting in *my* chair?" she asked in a medium-sized voice.

Then Baby Bear looked at his tiny, little chair. "Who has been sitting in *my* chair and broken it?" he asked in a tiny, little voice.

Next the three bears went into the bedroom. Father Bear looked at his very big bed. "Who has been lying on *my* bed?" he asked in a very loud voice.

Mother Bear looked at her medium-sized bed. "Who has been lying on *my* bed?" she asked in a medium-sized voice.

Baby Bear looked at his tiny, little bed.

"Here she is!" he cried, making his tiny, little voice as loud as he could. "Here is the naughty girl who has eaten *my* porridge and broken *my* chair! Here she is!"

At the sounds of their voices, Goldilocks woke up. When she saw the three bears she jumped off the bed in fright. She rushed to the window, jumped outside and ran quickly into the wood.

By the time the three bears reached the window, Goldilocks was out of sight. The three bears never saw her again.